Buster on the Farm

by Marc Brown

LITTLE, BROWN AND COMPANY

New York ᴥ Boston

Little, Brown and Company, Time Warner Book Group

1271 Avenue of the Americas, New York, NY 10020 • www.lb-kids.com

First Edition

Library of Congress Cataloging-in-Publication Data

Brown, Marc Tolon.

Buster on the farm / Marc Brown.—1st ed.   p. cm.—(Postcards from Buster)

Summary: Buster sends postcards to his friends back home when he goes to visit a farm in Indiana.

ISBN 0-316-15884-4 (hc)/ISBN 0-316-00108-2 (pb)

[1. Farm life—Indiana—Fiction. 2. Rabbits—Fiction. 3. Postcards—Fiction. 4. Indiana—Fiction.] I. Title. II. Series: Brown, Marc Tolon. Postcards from Buster. PZ7.B81618Bk 2005 [E]—dc22   2004010269

Printed in the United States of America • 10 9 8 7 6 5 4 3 2 1

Page 3: Fred M. Holycross ©1999. Other photos from *Postcards from Buster* courtesy of WGBH Boston, and Cinar Productions, Inc., in association with Marc Brown Studios.

Do you know what these words MEAN?

bale: to cut, press together, and tie up hay so that it can be stacked or stored

county: an area in a state that has its own government

county fair: a place where farm animals and products are shown to the public; often county fairs include amusement park rides, shows, and contests.

field: an area of cleared land that can be used for planting

hay: grasses that have been cut and dried

scarecrow: a life-sized figure that resembles a person and is used to scare birds away from crops

view: what you see from one place

STATE*tistics*

Indiana

- Indiana is the 19th state.
- There are 85,000 farms in Indiana.
- People from Indiana are known as "Hoosiers" (HOO-zhurz). No one is sure where the word came from. One theory is that when a visitor knocked on the door of a pioneer cabin in Indiana, the settler would respond, "Who's yere?")

Buster was going to visit
a farm in Indiana.

"You're so lucky,"
Arthur told him.

"I'll send lots of postcards,"
Buster promised.
"And I'll get everything
on film."

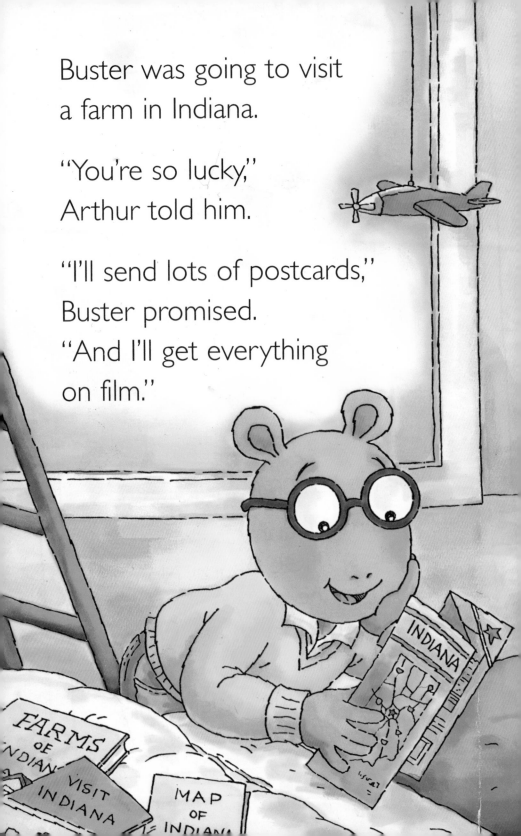

On the plane,
Buster kept staring
out the window.

"The farms sure look small,"
he thought.

Dear Arthur,

The farm is huge!

The horses are, too.

My new friend Lauren wants me to ride one.

No way!

Buster

Arthur Read
100 Main Street
Elwood Cit

Lauren showed Buster
around the farm.

He liked everyone he met—even
the scarecrow.

Dear Binky,

I rode on this tractor today.

It can cut down a field of corn in a few hours.

The tractor rumbles louder than your stomach before lunch.

Buster

At the henhouse,
Buster gathered some eggs.

"This is harder than buying them
at a store," he said.
"But more fun, too."

He laid the warm eggs
carefully in a basket.

The next morning
Buster went downstairs.

The sun wasn't up yet—
but Lauren was.

"Hey, Sleepyhead,"
she joked.
"The cows are waiting."

Francine Frensky
Maple ~~Drive~~ Apt. 5
Elwo~~~

Buster was busy all day.

First, he helped bale some hay.

Then he and Lauren
fed the animals
and cleaned the barn.

"Whew!" said Buster.
"Farming is hard work."

The next day all the chores were done early.

Then everyone got ready for the county fair.

"Don't worry, Buster," said Lauren. "Stay close to me and you won't get lost."

Dear Francine,

This is Francine.

Don't worry, she is not named after you.

We took her to the county fair.

Did you know that pigs are smarter than humans?

Buster

P.S. Don't tell the horses.

Buster could see the whole fair
from the top of the Ferris wheel.

"I wonder if the pigs
would like this view,"
he thought.

Buster couldn't believe
the next day was his
last day on the farm.

"I sure did a lot
on this trip," he said.

"There's one more thing
for you to do," said Lauren.

"What's that?" asked Buster.

"Take a horseback ride!"
said Lauren.

Dear Arthur,

I rode a horse!

Can you believe it?

It's a little like
riding a bike.

Only with
no handlebars.
And no brakes!

See you soon,
Buster

At last it was time to go.
Buster said good-bye.

"The cows will be waiting,"
said Lauren.

Dear Lauren,

Thanks for showing me your farm.

Someday we'll have to get your Francine to meet my Francine.

Your friend,
Sleepyhead
(Buster)